STUART SQUIRREL
LEARNS A LESSON

Written by Sandra D. Aldrich

Illustrated by Ryan Webb

Sandra D Aldrich

Celtic Cat Publishing
Knoxville, Tennessee

Printed in the United States of America

22 21 20 19 18 17   1 2 3 4 5 6 7 8 9 10

ISBN-13: 978-1-947020-00-9 (paper)

Library of Congress PCN: 2017939515

Aldrich, Sandra D.—Stuart Squirrel Learns a Lesson / Sandra D. Aldrich

Illustrated by Ryan Webb

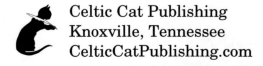

Celtic Cat Publishing
Knoxville, Tennessee
CelticCatPublishing.com

Foreword by Ranger Kim DeLozier

What is a bear worth? Without thinking, some might say, oh... not too much while others might say a bear is priceless. Okay, what about a deer, a turkey or even a squirrel? Some people think that wild animals will always be out there. Maybe they will, then again maybe not! We all—yes that means you too—have a responsibility to conserve and protect all of God's wild creatures on earth. Did you know in earlier times there were so many passenger pigeons that when they flew over the sky, it looked black from the thousands and thousands of birds?

Guess what? Today, there are no passenger pigeons. What happened? There were so many that the bird had no worth or value to the people and were not protected. The passenger pigeon is gone forever.

So, how do we protect other wild animals for the enjoyment of those after us? The answer is simple: just keep them wild. By helping them keep their natural fear of us, they generally do well. You might ask how we can do this. Part of our job is to keep people food and garbage away from wildlife.

Exposure to people food and garbage causes them to lose their fear of people and places their life in danger. Animals with little or no fear of people have an increased chance of being injured or killed by a car, shot by a poacher or even die from eating something bad in the garbage. I spent more than 30 years as a wildlife ranger at Great Smoky Mountains National Park trying to protect the animals by keeping people food and garbage away from bears, deer, elk, turkeys, and squirrels. It's a battle but wildlife is worth it.

In the story of Stuart the Squirrel, you will see how Stuart chooses the easy way of finding food while learning that going the easy route is not always best. Unfortunately, Stuart had to find out the hard way. The author does a great job of illustrating through the story of Stuart the potential danger of wild animals getting human food along with the associated consequences.

The message in Stuart the Squirrel applies not only to children but adults as well. By educating our children to keep the wild in wildlife, they will hopefully grow up and become the future educator for others. Stuart's story is a great start in spreading the word that people should eat people food and wild animals should eat wild foods.

I am sure that Stuart now understands why.

– E. Kim DeLozier
Supervisory, Wildlife Biologist (Retired)
Great Smoky Mountains National Park

Conservation Program Manager
Rocky Mountain Elk Foundation

Best-Selling Author, *Bear In The Back Seat*

Seymour, Tennessee

Dedication

This story is dedicated to the Principles of Leave No Trace and all the rangers and volunteers who promote these important principles to help keep our national parks protected so as future generations will be able to enjoy these majestic places we are so lucky to have!

Ranger Christine Hoyer is an amazing ranger who loves what she does and is amazing at accomplishing it. Her compassion about teaching us the principles of Leave No Trace was contagious. If it wasn't for her, Stuart Squirrel Learns a Lesson wouldn't have been written!

Acknowledgements

I want to thank my husband, Jay, for his wonderful patience and understanding while I worked on this book. He has been with me through all of my stories and has helped me tremendously.

My daughter, Ellen Holly, has helped me with proofreading Stuart since the beginning. Her talent and eye for finding any grammatical and spelling errors that I may have overlooked, is amazing! Thank you, Ellen.

I also want to thank my son, Benjamin and daughter-in-law, Laura, for their support. Their encouragement was contagious in this journey of being an author!

Stuart Red Squirrel loved living in the Great Smoky Mountains National Park. His family had lived here for generations and generations. He couldn't believe how beautiful this park was!

Stuart's friends loved this park as well. They would play and romp around all day...

Except for school days of course.

His parents and teachers would go over the rules for safety almost every day. It seemed a waste of time to keep going over these safety rules so much; even his friends thought so! Really, what could happen to them in this wonderful park of theirs?

Monday's lesson was about eating only the food they were taught to eat since they were young. Since this year was a good year, there were plenty of acorns, nuts, seeds, and berries to keep their tummies full.

Stuart's teacher, Mrs. Reddish,
was talking once more about not
eating hikers' food or any food
that could have been dropped
on the ground.

Since the class listened so carefully, Mrs. Reddish let the class play Nut Burying and let them take part in drey building.

A drey, as Mrs. Reddish explained, is what squirrels call their nests. She wanted all the animals in her class to learn about how and where others live.

A few days later, Stuart Squirrel and Chester Chipmunk decided to go wandering. They would take turns playing hide and go seek in the forest.

Stuart hid in a hole in one of the tulip trees and Chester hid under the leaves of a pin cherry tree.

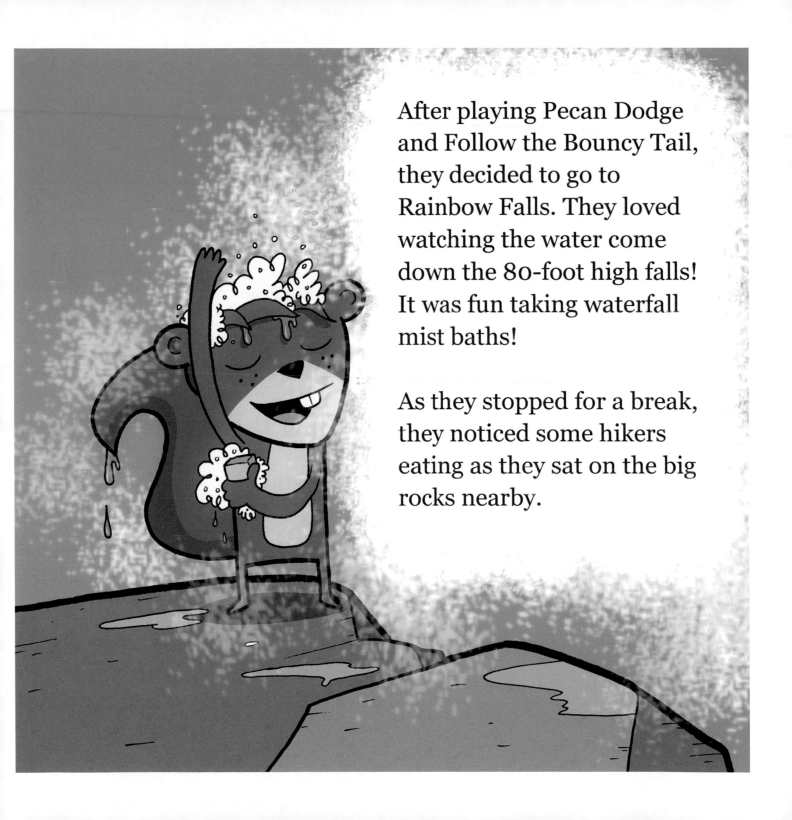

After playing Pecan Dodge and Follow the Bouncy Tail, they decided to go to Rainbow Falls. They loved watching the water come down the 80-foot high falls! It was fun taking waterfall mist baths!

As they stopped for a break, they noticed some hikers eating as they sat on the big rocks nearby.

"Oh boy Chester! Look at that food!" cried Stuart.

"No food from hikers, Stuart!" cried Chester. "You know what we have been taught about food from hikers!"

"Yeah, I know, but a little bit won't hurt us!" answered Stuart.

"NO! Now, let's go now!" replied Chester and finally Stuart followed him down the trail towards home.

When Stuart got home, his mom wanted to know what he did with Chester. He explained how they played hide and go seek and then went to Rainbow Falls where they saw some hikers.

"You didn't eat any of their food did you?" asked his mom.

"No, we left, but I still don't get why we can't eat what they eat!" exclaimed Stuart.

"Stuart, I have told you and so has Mrs. Reddish. It can make you sick! You know that we worry about you and tell you these things because we love you! Now go wash up for dinner!" said Mrs. Squirrel.

Stuart listened to his mom and ate his dinner.
Soon it was time for bed.

Stuart thought about all the food those
hikers had, and bet if the hikers
had seen him and Chester,
they could have gotten some.

Since it was the weekend, Stuart decided to go on a long hike by himself. He hiked over to the Elkmont Campground. Stuart loved going to the Elkmont Campground. There was a river he could drink from and just maybe, he could find some of that food that campers leave behind.

He was tired after all that running to get there. After resting a bit, Stuart decided to search for some of that human food he hoped he would find. He looked around one of the campsites, but didn't see any. Stuart did find some acorns though, so he sat and started to eat a few.

A short time later, Stuart noticed a little boy who was eating a sandwich at a picnic table. Stuart decided to go up to him.

It wasn't that Stuart forgot what he was taught in school and what his mother told him about eating people food; he just knew it looked so good and if this little boy could eat it, why not him? After all, it smelled just like some of the nuts that were in the park, so it had to be okay!

Stuart ran over to the little boy whose name was Tommy.

Stuart looked up at Tommy and started to chatter,
"I'm Stuart and I sure would like whatever you have! I get
tired of acorns and seeds. I see hikers eating things other
than these old seeds and acorns."

The little boy just looked at him and didn't understand what Stuart was trying to say. He figured that Stuart was just begging for some of his peanut butter and jelly sandwich.

Tommy thought if he gave Stuart some of his sandwich, then maybe he would play fetch with him. He put some of the food down on the ground and Stuart gobbled it up. When Stuart finished eating, Tommy threw his ball and watched Stuart get it. Stuart decided to get Tommy to play squirrel games, but Tommy didn't understand. Just then, Tommy's mother called and said it was time to get back to the tent.

'I hope I get to see you again!" Tommy called as he left.

Stuart started running home.
When he reached his nest in the
tall fir tree, his tummy was really hurting!

"What's wrong?" Stuart's mom asked as he came up the tree. "Did you fall and hurt yourself?"

"No, I ate this little piece of food that tasted like peanuts that this little boy shared with me and now I don't feel so good!" cried Stuart.

"Now Stuart, you know we told you not to eat people food, but I understand. When I was a little girl, I was curious about human food, so I tasted some and I liked it. But, like you, my tummy started to hurt. That is why Mrs. Reddish and I tell you not to eat anything but your own food."

Mrs. Squirrel felt his head and had him lie down on his soft leafy bed. "I know you have a tummy ache, I also know just the thing for that," Mrs. Red Squirrel said and she gave him a kiss on his head.

"I'll be right back," she said as she left the room. Stuart snuggled down in his bed and waited for mom.

"Here is some herbal tea that will make your tummy feel better," Mom said as she handed Stuart the warm mug. Stuart fell fast asleep as soon as he finished it.

The next day in school, Stuart had volunteered to stand up in front of his class and explain what happened when he ate food from humans.

"I have learned my lesson! Don't eat human food and don't try to talk or play with humans, ever! They don't understand when you try to talk to them anyway! I promise never to eat **anything** people bring into the woods ever again!"

DON'T EAT HUMAN FOOD!

We know that animals really can't talk and teach their children not to eat the food that people eat, so we must learn the lesson for them. When you go to any National Park you must never feed the animals!

Remember:
We must LEAVE NO TRACE
of our visit!

Leave No Trace

Stuart learned the hard way about not eating food that humans eat. Tommy didn't know about the LEAVE NO TRACE principle that states:

"Respect Wildlife!"

You can help the wildlife in the parks by folllowing that principle. Observe animals from a distance and NEVER APPROACH, FEED, OR FOLLOW THEM! Human food is UNHEALTHY for all animals and feeding them starts bad habits. Protect wildlfe and your food by storing your meals and trash. CONTROL PETS at all times, or leave them at home.

Seven Principles of Leave No Trace

1. Plan Ahead and Prepare

2. Travel and Camp on Durable Surfaces

3. Dispose of Waste Properly

4. Leave What You Find

5. Minimize Campfire Impacts

6. Respect Wildlife

7. Be Considerate of other Visitors

The Leave No Trace Center for Outdoor Ethics also has derivations of the principles that correspond with various activities and and environments such as Frontcountry, Kids, Heritage Sites, River Corridors, Fishing, Urban, Climbing, Hunting, and International.

The member-driven Leave No Trace Center for Outdoor Ethics teaches people how to enjoy the outdoors responsibly. This copyrighted information has been reprinted with permission from the Leave No Trace Center for Outdoor Ethics: www.LNT.org

Some Interesting Facts about the Great Smoky Mountains National Park

- In 1934 the Great Smoky Mountains National Park was established. It is the largest national park east of the Rocky Mountains.

- The park encloses 522,427 acres in both North Carolina and Tennessee.

- The park is opened 24 hours a day and 365 days a year. Some secondary roads, visitor facilities, and campgrounds are closed in the winter.

- The Great Smoky Mountains National Park is the most visited national park in the United States. It has 10-11 million visitors a year and has no entrance fee.

- There is a 32-mile stretch of road that connects Gatlinburg, Tennessee, to Cherokee, North Carolina via Newfound Gap Road (US441). The road offers vistas, picnic areas, rivers, and mountain streams. Park guests can go into the Sugarland and Oconaluftee visitor centers.

- A 70-mile stretch of the 2,178 mile Appalachian Trail goes through the Great Smoky Mountains National Park.

- Cades Cove is a 4,000-acre valley that has a campground, hiking trails, preserved homesteads, and churches. It is the most visited part of the park. Black bears, foxes, wild turkeys, deer, and raccoons call Cades Cove their home. The best time to see them is dawn or dusk.

- Visitors can view a typical Smoky Mountains homestead, with a barn, corncrib, smokehouse, and blacksmith shop, near the Abrams Falls parking area in Cades Cove.

- In 1976, the park was designated an International Biosphere Reserve, because of its biodiversity. Biodiversity means the variety of plants and animals in the park. The Smoky Mountains National Park has over 19,000 kinds of plants and animals!

- Groundhog, red fox, coyote, eastern cottontail rabbit, bobcat, river otter, white-tailed deer, and wild boar are just some of the animals that inhabit the Great Smoky Mountains National Park.

- Popular activities in the Great Smoky Mountains National Park include fishing, hiking, camping, and quiet nature walks.

- A few favorite hiking trails are: Alum Cave Trail (11 miles round trip), Abrams Falls Trail (5 miles round trip), Boulevard Trail (16 miles round trip), Andrews Bald Trail (3.6 miles round trip, Grotto Falls (3 miles round trip), Chimney Tops (4 miles round trip), Laurel Falls (2.5 miles round trip), Ramsey Cascades Trail (8 miles round trip), and Sugarlands Valley Nature Trail, a 3,000-foot loop.

- Including the miles of the Appalachian Trail that wind through the park, there are more than 850 miles of hiking trails.

Information from nps.gov

71182503R00022

Made in the USA
Columbia, SC
25 May 2017